WAGON TRAIN

A Family Goes West in 1865

by Courtni C. Wright

illustrated by Gershom Griffith

Holiday House/New York

To my cousin Alma, Aunt Virginia, and Uncle Leslie
—C.C. Wright

For my brothers, David and Anderson,
and my sisters, Marjorie and Alene
—Gershom Griffith

Text copyright © 1995 by Courtni C. Wright
Illustrations copyright © 1995 by Gershom Griffith
ALL RIGHTS RESERVED
Printed in the United States of America
FIRST EDITION

Library of Congress Cataloging-in-Publication Data
Wright, Courtni Crump.
Wagon train: a family goes west in 1865 / Courtni
C. Wright: illustrated by Gershom Griffith.—1st ed.
p.   cm.
ISBN 0-8234-1152-4
1. Afro-American pioneers—West (U.S.)—History—19th century—
—Juvenile literature.   2. Overland journeys to the Pacific—Juvenile
literature.   3. West (U.S.)—History—1860-1890—Juvenile
literature.   [1. Afro-Americans—History—1863-1877.   2. Overland
journeys to the Pacific.   3. Frontier and pioneer life.   4. West
(U.S.)—History—1860-1890.]   I. Griffith, Gershom, ill.
II. Title.
E185.925.W75   1995   94-18975   CIP   AC
978′.00496073—dc20

AUTHOR'S NOTE

Just as white Americans traveled to the West looking for land, gold, religious freedom, a new life, and excitement, so too did African-Americans before and after the Civil War. Many escaped to Kansas and California, hoping to find freedom and safety from oppression. Others went hunting for the riches of gold. Whatever their goal, they found prejudice, bigotry, and poor living and working conditions. Their lives were hard in the West but less so than if they remained in slavery or starved in the war-ravaged South.

We will never really know what happened to the thousands of African-Americans who made the four- to five-month trip along the Oregon Trail because few could write diaries to record their experiences for us. History tells us that their trip was long and hard and that many died. People and oxen starved to death in the cruel wilderness when winter's snows trapped them in the mountains without food and shelter. Those who survived often watched helplessly as their wagons toppled over mountainsides, their few possessions lost forever. Regardless of the hardships, the promise of the West called to them.

In a picture book, it is impossible to depict everything that Ginny's family might have experienced on its pilgrimage to the West. My desire here was simply to share with you a few episodes from their fictional journey.

—*Courtni C. Wright*

The sun is bright the day we leave the plantation in Virginia. The Civil War is over. Daffodils and tulips are blooming in the garden, and bees are buzzing in the crab apple trees that line the road.

My name is Virginia, but everyone calls me Ginny. Mistress named me for the Commonwealth of Virginia. Some of the other slaves are named for states, too. There is a Georgia and a Carolina. After we get to California, I think I'll call myself Callie.

Before leaving the plantation, we pick the garden behind the slave quarters clean. Ma, Pa, my brother Ben, and I roll up our old straw-stuffed pallets and load them into the wagon. We pack everything we need for the trip, then we close the door to the cabin. We will never return. This row of tiny shacks behind the big house will never be home to us again.

Grandma Sadie raises her hands to the sky and shouts, "Praise the Lord! Thank you, Jesus! We's finally leavin' this here place!" She is eighty-three years old and has been a slave all her life.

The wagon will be our home until we reach California. It is not very large. We do not have many things to carry. Pa made a small table, three wooden stools, and a cradle for Molly, my new baby sister. She was born three weeks ago. We will use the stools around the campfire and later in our new house. Ma is bringing along the old iron kettle for cooking and an oak rocking chair for rocking the baby to sleep. Ben is not bringing anything except his slingshot.

I am bringing my only corncob doll, Chrissy. I cannot leave her behind in the slave quarters. She would be lonely without me. Pa made her in the fall after he finished harvesting the tobacco. Ma made a striped dress for her from some scraps of material. She even made a blue calico bonnet for Chrissy's head.

"Hurry, Ginny! We's leavin'!" Ben shouts as I take one last look around the quarters.

Before freedom came, Pa did not live with us. We lived on Master John's plantation, and Pa lived on a neighboring one. He came to visit us on Sundays if his master gave him a traveling pass. Ma was always afraid she would hear he had been sold down South.

There are twelve wagons in the train. We used to all be slaves on this plantation or the one where Pa lived. We worked together in the tobacco fields and in the cookhouse. We ate together in the quarters and shared everything we had. Now, we are traveling together. Grandpa William is riding with us. He is probably the oldest person on the plantation. The wagon master, Mr. Turner, shouts for each wagon to stay in line behind the one in front of it. He does not want anyone to get lost.

Before the war, we saved up money from the sale of crops grown in the little gardens behind the quarters. We used it to buy cloth, chickens, and, with luck, freedom. Now that the war is over and we are free, Ma and Pa spent it for the covered wagon, the horses and food supplies, and to pay Mr. Turner and his scout.

In the days before freedom, slaves would walk behind their master's wagon on the long trip to the West, tending the cows. We were not allowed to ride because the law said we were not equal to white people. Today, we still cannot join one of the big trains leaving Independence, Missouri. Many white people want us to stay apart from them, so we formed our own train.

Ma is very excited about the trip West. She talks all the time about starting a new life in the house Pa will build. She says it will have a sleeping loft for us kids and a bedroom for them. It will have wooden shutters, not rags blowing in the breeze. She says there will be a real wood floor, too. The one in the slave cabin was hard-packed dirt. It was always cold in the winter. Water oozed up into the cabin after a heavy rain in the spring. Pa says I will have a real bed, not just a straw-stuffed pallet. He says we will raise chickens, pigs, and cows, too.

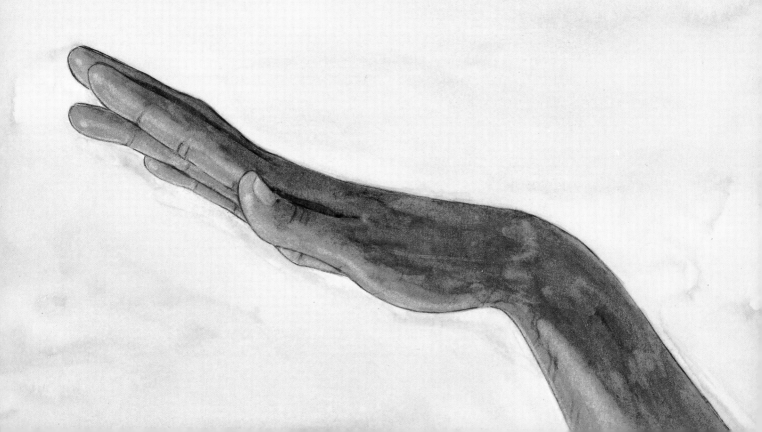

The wagon is small and rocks from side to side on the bumpy road. It is pulled by a team of four horses. Pa will sell the horses and buy four oxen when we reach Independence. They are stronger for the rugged Oregon Trail. When we get to California, Pa will use two of them on the farm to help him plow the land. The others will be sold to buy corn for planting, and cows and chickens.

Ben and I walk behind the wagon as much as possible. On the plantation, we worked from sunup to sundown in the big house or the field with hardly any time to rest. It would be hard for us to sit for a long time.

Now we have reached Independence and are on the Oregon Trail. It took over a month to get here on the Cumberland Road. The wheel on Miss Bessie's wagon broke and had to be mended as we traveled through the Appalachian Mountains. The mountains smelled of pine and new leaves. Laurel and rhododendrons bloomed everywhere. Water glistened in the creeks and rivers along the way. Ben and I ran in and out of the trees until I got poison ivy on my legs. After that, we stayed on the road.

Pa was afraid we'd lose our wagon when we crossed the Missouri River. Ma held us close in her arms. We said a prayer of thanks when we safely reached the other side.

Mr. Turner says, "You best prepare yourselves for some rough going. The Rockies and Sierra Nevadas don't have smooth roads."

"Don't fret yourself, Mr. Turner. We make it just fine. We was slaves, remember. Hard times mean nothin' to us," Pa replies with a sad smile.

Every night when it starts to get dark, the wagon master tells us to make a circle with the wagons. The older boys and men take turns watching for Indians, while the women fix dinner. The children help out by gathering wood for the fire and water from the nearby stream. We sing and play tag after we eat, if we are not too tired. We go to sleep early because we wake up with the first rays of the sun. We travel at least fifteen miles each day and cannot be slug-a-beds.

The sky seems darker here than in Virginia, and the stars look brighter. They twinkle like fireflies in the indigo sky. Last night we saw a shooting star streak through the heavens. Grandma Sadie said it was good luck.

This Sunday, we do not travel. Grandpa William leads us in a short prayer service and hymn singing in the morning. Pa's voice fills the mountains as he sings "Many Thousand Gone."

> *No more mistress call for me,*
> *No more, no more,—*
> *No more mistress call for me,*
> *Many thousand go.*

Tears are in everyone's eyes when he reaches the last verse. Everyone thinks about the hard days of slavery and the many who died without ever tasting freedom.

Later, we do our chores. The children gather wood for the cook-fire. Pa and the other men make repairs on the wagons and oxen harnesses. The women wash clothes in the stream and pick wild berries.

Today, while Pa and Ben grease the axle on the wagon, Ma and I take the wash down to the stream. Ma pounds the shirts, pants, and dresses on the stones to remove the dust and dirt of the trail. When they are clean, she gives them to me. I hang them on low tree limbs to dry in the hot sun.

I help by watching over Molly, too. She sleeps in a twig basket covered with a thin white sheet to keep out the sun.

After we finish washing the last shirt, Ben comes running toward us. "Ma, come quick! Pa's been bit by a snake!" he shouts. Quickly, he turns and runs back to the wagon, leaving a cloud of dust.

"Ginny, you brings Molly. I's gonna see what I can do," Ma says as she gathers up her long skirts. Holding Molly's basket in one hand and my doll in the other, I follow her.

Pa is sitting with his back against the rear wheel of the wagon. His face is ashy. He has cut his pants leg up to the knee and has used a handkerchief as a tourniquet to keep the snake poison from spreading. Four red, angry holes show on the muscle of his left calf.

"'Twas a rattler, Mary. Got away, too, 'fore I can shoot it. I stepped back to look at the wheel. Didn't see it until it was too late. Got me good," Pa says as the sweat rolls down his forehead and glistens on his cheeks.

"What you wants me to do, Tom? You knows there ain't no doctor on the wagon train. Mr. Turner and his scout out searchin' for water. I can suck out the poison the way I seen him do when Ol' Moss got bit," offers Ma.

"I reckon that's the only way, Mary. Ben, get the whiskey from the wagon. Your ma needs it for washin' the bite," Pa orders.

"Give me your knife. We gots to do this quick 'fore the poison spreads too far," Ma says, taking the knife in her trembling hand.

"I's ready. Do it fast," whispers Pa. He grits his teeth as he waits for the pain of the blade.

Ma sits on the dusty ground beside him. The bite is red and swelling fast. She takes the knife and quietly looks into Pa's drawn face.

"You chil'ren get in the wagon," she tells us. "Ben, help Ginny lift the baby's basket inside. I don't want y'all seein' this. Pull that flap closed tight, ya hear?"

"Yes, ma'am," Ben answers. He takes the basket and leads me to the wagon.

"Pa be all right, won't he?" I ask, as Ben helps me up.

"Don't worry. Ma take good care of him." Ben tries to sound brave, but he is worried, too. I know when something is bothering him because he chews on his bottom lip. Ben is chewing on it now. We leave the wagon flap open a bit so we can see what Ma is doing.

She quickly cuts an X in the wound. Pa grunts softly as the blade pierces his flesh. The blood wells in the cut. Ma puts her mouth over it and sucks. She sucks and spits until her cheeks are tired. She has to be sure all the poison is gone.

Then she pours some whiskey from the little brown jug onto Pa's calf. It burns as it mixes with the blood, but he does not cry out. Instead, he clenches his teeth even tighter.

"I done my best, Tom. I prays I got it all," Ma says as she tears off a piece of her petticoat and wraps it around his calf.

"You done good, Mary. No doctor coulda done better," Pa tells her as he wipes the sweat from his forehead. "Help me up. I gots to finish greasin' that axle," he adds.

Pa limps slowly toward the wagon. He sticks his head inside and says, "I'm fine, chil'ren. Hop down and help your ma gather firewood. We done had enough excitement for one day, and I's hungry."

"Yes, Pa," Ben answers. We scurry off to look for twigs, brush, and buffalo chips.

That night, we eat rabbit stew seasoned with some of the wild onions and flowers that grow in the meadow. Pa is not feeling well from the snakebite. He only eats a little.

The next morning we are up early. Pa walks with a slight limp and is very tired. He says he is feeling well enough to travel, though. As we head out, Pa tells us the wagon master said that we should reach the Sierra Nevadas in about two months.

The wagons in the train are traveling closer together now. We circle tighter at night, too. Puffs of dust appear often in the distance. Pa keeps a lookout for Indians and buffalo. There is always someone on watch. Mr. Turner says the Indians will not hurt us. They want to be left alone to live in peace. They are angry that the government has ordered them to live on reservations where the land is too poor to grow crops.

One morning, as Pa is hitching up the horses, Ma sees a cloud of dust moving toward us. It comes closer, and we hear the cries of Indians. Quickly, Pa grabs his rifle and crouches behind some barrels.

"Get under the wagon, children," Ma shouts as she pushes Molly's basket ahead of us.

Five Indians on horseback ride up to the wagon train. They are wearing woven breechcloth at their waists, shirts with fringe hanging from the elbows, and striped moccasins. They carry rifles, too. They have painted their faces in colorful lines and patterns. Mr. Turner thinks they are Arapaho.

The Indians ride around the wagons, waving their rifles and shouting. Molly begins to whimper. I rock her slowly, and she quiets down. Ben whispers, "Don't you worry, Ginny. I's protects you and Molly. Nobody gonna hurt you as long as I's here." He sounds brave, but Ben is chewing his lip.

Suddenly, they stop shouting. One of them dismounts and walks toward the wagons, holding a crooked lance in his hand. Mr. Turner walks out to meet him, carrying a sack of sugar. They talk for a long time. Before the Indians ride away, the warrior hands him a bundle of dried buffalo meat. It is very chewy and tough but not too different from the venison we used to eat on the plantation.

Mr. Turner says the Indians were a scouting party looking for food. They say they found water over the ridge about a mile from here. We hurry to hitch up the horses and load the last of our belongings. The promise of something cool to drink and a place to wash makes all of us work faster. Soon, we are traveling in the direction the Indian warrior pointed.

Ben is the first one to dip his hands in the cool, clear water. For a long time, I cannot move. I sit and look at the river as it flows past. It sparkles like a rainbow in the sunlight and drips from Ben's fingers as he drinks in big noisy gulps.

"Climb down, Ginny," Ben calls between swallows. "This here's the best water I ever tasted!"

Ben is right, the water is wonderful. Fish jump and splash as I wash my face. I giggle as the cool drops slide down my neck.

We make camp by the river early tonight. The coyotes come to drink in the moonlight as the bats fly overhead. The air smells clean and cool, but the sandy ground is still warm from the scorching sun.

The next day we begin our journey again. Our water barrels are full and we are rested. We have slept well beside the gentle rippling of the river.

The weeks pass and lengthen into months. The land is flat and dry with only sagebrush and cactus. Snakes slither by in the distance. Lizards sit on rocks along the side of the road. Their tongues dart like lightning to catch passing bugs. There is very little water left in the barrel Pa filled at the river. Ma worries that we will not find more. Baby Molly does not cry much now. It is too hot for her, even in the shade of the wagon's cover.

Mr. Turner sends his scout ahead to search for water as we travel through the desert. Everyone hopes he will return soon with good news. The sun is hot and the nights are cool. The howling of the coyotes and the hooting of the owls fill the stillness. There is no path to follow, and everything looks the same. Only the wagon master seems to know where we are going.

Sometimes, I think we will never reach California. The sun beats down on our heads all day. The bonnet Ma makes me wear does not help much. The seat in the wagon is hard. My backside is sore from bumping over the rocks. I cannot walk behind the wagon now; I am too tired and thirsty.

Ben is tired of traveling, too. He never complains, but he chews his lip all the time now. Ma has dark circles under her eyes. Pa's beard is red with trail dust. We are always thirsty and dirty. There is no way to keep the dust and grit out of our food and eyes.

It is as cold now as it was hot only a few days ago. We are wrapped up in blankets, and still I shiver. No one rides in the wagons. The trail through the Sierra Nevadas is too steep and treacherous. Remains of broken wagons line the path. Mr. Turner says he has seen them tumble down the mountainside. Pa walks in front of the oxen, pulling them along. Ma, Grandpa William, and Ben walk behind, prodding them. Coming down will be just as hard. I carry Molly in my arms. She has outgrown her basket.

Late one afternoon, I lay my head on Ma's shoulder and try to take a nap as I ride on the hard wagon seat. Pa whistles a dry little tune as he flicks the reins against the oxen's backs. As I fall asleep, I hear Mr. Turner ride past on his horse. He stops to say something to Ma and Pa. I struggle to open my eyes as he shouts, "Look over there, beyond the trees! California's round the bend."

I rub my eyes and look past his pointing finger. There, in the clouds and gray of the far-away distance, past the purple mounds of hills, are fuzzy green valleys.

"Pa, is it really California?" I ask, tugging on Pa's shirt.

Ben has been riding in the back with Molly and Grandpa William. At the sound of voices, he sticks his head out and asks, "Is we there yet?"

Pa puts his arms around us and says in a slow quiet voice, "Yes, chil'ren, that California all right. We done made it. We's home."

"Praise the Lord!" Grandpa William shouts.

A tear slips slowly down Ma's cheek.

California! Our new home is just over the hills. Now the work of building a new life really begins.